Topsy and Tim
Go Camping

By Jean and Gareth Adamson

Illustrations by Belinda Worsley

A catalogue record for this book is available from the British Library

This title was previously published as part of the Topsy and Tim Learnabout series
Published by Ladybird Books Ltd
A Penguin Company
Penguin Books Ltd., 80 Strand, London WC2R 0RL, UK
Penguin Books Australia Ltd., Camberwell, Victoria, Australia
Penguin Group (NZ) 67 Apollo Drive, Rosedale, North Shore 0632, New Zealand

002 – 3 5 7 9 10 8 6 4 2

ISBN: 978-1-40930-333-6
Printed in China

www.topsyandtim.com

This Topsy and Tim book belongs to

_____

Topsy and Tim were going camping with
Mummy and Dad. They were taking two
tents – a big one for Mummy and Dad and
a small one for Topsy and Tim.

It was a long drive, but at last they arrived at the campsite. It was in a field, beside a little wood. Topsy and Tim helped to unload the car.

Putting the tents up was a puzzle
at first, but Topsy and Tim soon
remembered how to do it.
"I like our tent best," said Topsy.

Tim went to fetch water. He was surprised to find a tap in the field. It was a very splashy tap.

There was hot soup for supper and sandwiches
and big red apples.

After supper, Topsy and Tim went with Mummy
and Dad to explore the wood.
"Somebody's been painting arrows on the trees,"
said Tim. "Look!"

"Yes," said Mummy. "If we follow those arrows, they will take us for a good walk and bring us back to camp."

When they got back to their camp they saw that another family had arrived in the field – two big boys and their mum and dad. They were unloading their car and putting up their tent.

The big boys were very noisy.
"Let's go and play inside our tent," said Topsy to Tim.
"It's time you two got into your sleeping bags,"
said Mummy.

Topsy and Tim were almost asleep in their cosy sleeping
bags when something hit their tent with a WALLOP!
It gave them a fright.

The naughty boys had kicked a football
hard at Topsy and Tim's tent.
"Sorry," called the boys.

Next morning, Topsy and Tim were up bright and early
and so were the big boys.
"We are going to play in the wood," said the big boys.
"We'll come too," said Topsy and Tim.

They had a wonderful time in the wood.
They swung from trees like monkeys.
"I'm the king of the jungle!" shouted Tim.

They chased after rabbits, trying to catch them, but the rabbits ran faster.

"I nearly caught one," puffed Topsy, "but it ran down a rabbit hole."

At last they began to feel hungry. None of them
had had breakfast. They wanted to go back to the
camp, but they did not know which way to go.

"We're lost," said one of the big boys.
"No we're not," said Topsy.
"The arrows on the trees will lead us back
to camp. Mummy said so."

Mummy and Dad were glad to see them.
"I was just coming to find you," said Dad.
"What have you been up to?"
"We've had adventures," said Tim.

Topsy and Tim were ready for breakfast,
but Mummy could not get the camp stove to work.
"We'll have to make do with
a cold breakfast," she said.

The big boys' dad came to see what was wrong.
"Come and join us," he said. "There's plenty of
room on our barbeque."

Soon there was the lovely smell of sausages and bacon cooking on the big boys' barbeque – and there was plenty for everyone.

"I love camping," said Tim.
"I wish we could stay here forever," said Topsy.

Now turn the page and help
Topsy and Tim solve a puzzle.

Mummy, Dad, Topsy and Tim are having
supper at the campsite.
Look at the five jigsaw pieces.
Can you work out where each piece will fit?

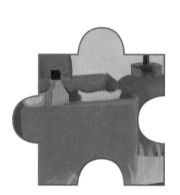

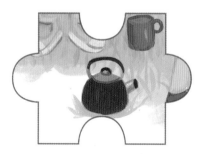

A Map of the Village

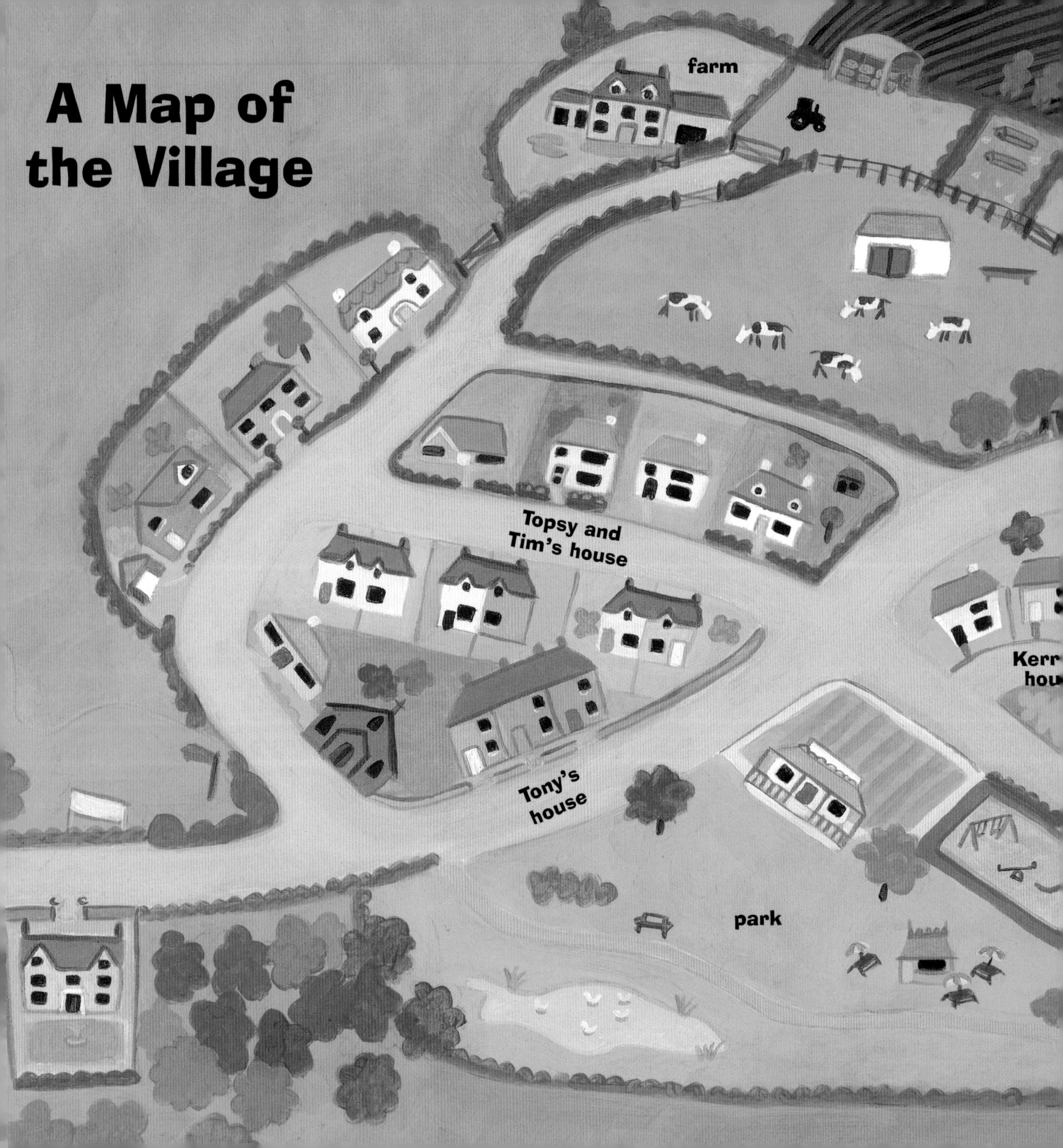

farm

Topsy and
Tim's house

Tony's
house

Kerr
hou

park

garage

health centre

post office

church

primary school

nursery school

police station

Look out for other titles in the series.